The Frog Princess

Retold as a Play by Frances Bacon
Illustrated by Helen Bacon

Russia

Anya loves seeing the beautiful palaces, cathedrals, and museums when she travels into Moscow with her family. She is proud to be from a country with such a rich history. She tries to imagine what it must have been like to be part of a Russian royal family, like the one in this story.

The Cast of Characters

 Narrator

 Olga

 Czar

 Frog Princess

 Peter

 Guest 1

 Marko

 Guest 2

 Ivan

 Vasilisa

 Sonya

 Baba-Yaga

In this play from Russia, we learn that even in the most difficult situations, kindness is often richly rewarded.

kindness helping others

Narrator: Long, long ago in Russia, there lived a czar and his three handsome sons. Their names were Peter, Marko, and Ivan. One day, the czar decided that it was time for his sons to marry.

Czar: I will give each of you an arrow. Shoot the arrow high into the air. Whoever finds the arrow will become your wife.

Narrator: Peter was the first to shoot his arrow. It skimmed over the ocean and landed on the deck of a large ship. Next, Marko shot his arrow. It flew over the mountains and came to rest in the garden of an important family. Last, it was Ivan's turn. Ivan's arrow wobbled through some trees and splashed into Baba-Yaga's swamp.

Czar: Well done, young princes. Now we will get ready for the wedding. I can't wait to see who your brides will be.

Narrator: On the day of the wedding, the czar and his three sons stood outside the palace. They did not have to wait for long.

Sonya: My name is Sonya. Peter's golden arrow landed on my father's ship. I am here to marry Peter.

Olga: My name is Olga. Marko's silver arrow landed in my family's garden. I am here to marry Marko.

Frog Princess: My name is Vasilisa.
Ribbit! Ribbit! Ivan's plain arrow landed in
Baba-Yaga's swamp. I am here to marry Ivan.

Ivan: Oh, no, you're not! Father, I cannot
marry a frog!

Czar: You have to, Ivan. That was the deal.
(Peter and Marko laugh.)

Narrator: Sonya rode to the church in a golden carriage. Olga traveled in a silver carriage. Frowning, Ivan walked with his frog bride, Vasilisa, hopping along behind him.

carriage a coach

9

Narrator: After a month, the czar called his sons together.

Czar: I have a test for your wives. I would like each of them to stitch this cloth into a shirt.

Sonya: (*grumbling*) When I picked up your golden arrow, Peter, no one said anything about sewing!

Olga: (*grumbling*) Who has ever heard of a princess making shirts? I'll try, Marko, but I'm not happy!

Narrator: Ivan did not have much hope as he lay the material down in front of Vasilisa. She jumped on the material and tore it into shreds.

stitch to sew

Ivan: How come my brothers got to marry beautiful princesses and I got stuck with an ugly frog? Vasilisa, you are just a stupid animal! *(Ivan runs from the room.)*

Narrator: Princess Sonya did try to make a shirt, but she had never sewn before. She cut one sleeve too long and one sleeve too short. Her seams were as wavy as rivers.

Peter: What is father going to say about this?

Narrator: Princess Olga did not do any better. She pricked her finger with the needle and shed spots of blood all over the shirt.

Marko: Don't cry. You're good at other things!

wavy wave-like curves

Narrator: Vasilisa, the frog princess, did not even pick up a needle. She threw the ripped pieces of cloth out the window and croaked. Suddenly, a perfectly made shirt flapped into the room and dropped at her feet.

The next morning, the czar asked to see the shirts. *(The three princesses give the czar their shirts.)*

Czar: Princess Sonya and Princess Olga, I see that you have tried, but I'm afraid your shirts are not nearly as beautiful as Vasilisa's.

Ivan: *(proud and surprised)* Maybe Vasilisa is not just a slimy old frog after all! *(To Vasilisa)* Come, my bride, let's go for a walk together. I'll wear the shirt you made!

13

Narrator: A second month passed, and the czar thought it was time for another test.

Czar: I would like each of you to bake a loaf of bread.

Sonya: *(whispering to Olga)* Let's hide and watch Vasilisa make her bread. I know she's up to something.

Narrator: The two princesses watched Vasilisa at work. First, she sprinkled flour on the floor like snow. Next, she broke some eggs on the floor and spilled a bucket of water. Then Vasilisa used a broom to sweep the sticky mess into a bread pan, and finally she pushed the pan into the oven.

Olga: That is the strangest way to make bread, but if it works for Vasilisa, it should work for us. Here are the eggs, Sonya. Throw them on the floor.

Narrator: Sonya and Olga copied everything Vasilisa had done. Then they gave their loaves to the czar.

Czar: Yuck! Your bread is as hard as a brick.

Olga and Sonya: Oh, no! Now that slimy Vasilisa will win this contest as well!

Czar: Your bread is delicious, Vasilisa. Well done.

Ivan: You are very talented, my dear Vasilisa.

Narrator: A third month passed, and the czar decided to hold a ball for everyone in the city.

Czar: Good people of my kingdom, I would like to present to you Princess Sonya, Princess Olga, and Princess Vasilisa. (*Sonya and Olga step forward to greet the ball guests. There is no sign of Vasilisa.*)

Guest 1: Princess Sonya and Princess Olga are both very beautiful, but where is Princess Vasilisa? People are saying that she is strange.

Guest 2: I have heard that she is a frog!

Narrator: Suddenly, a beautiful young woman walked into the room. Nobody knew who she was.

Czar: (*kneeling*) Please join us, my lady.

Vasilisa: Do you not know who I am, dear Father? I am Vasilisa, Ivan's frog princess.

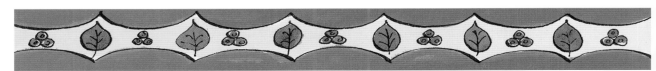

Czar: Goodness me! Well, Vasilisa, would you give me the honor of a dance?

Narrator: The czar and Vasilisa danced to one song after another. The crowd clapped—except for Peter, Marko, and their wives. They were too jealous.

Peter: Ivan, this beautiful princess can't be your wife. Where is your ugly frog bride?

Ivan: I don't know, but I'm going to find out!

Narrator: Prince Ivan went down to the kitchen. When he got there, he saw the green skin of a frog lying on the floor. Ivan picked it up and threw it into the fire.

Vasilisa: (*entering kitchen*) There you are, Ivan. I've been looking for you. (*sniffing*) Is something burning?

Ivan: It's your old frog skin! I've gotten rid of it.

Vasilisa: Oh, no! Long ago, my father had me changed from a princess into a frog. I was allowed to be a princess for only one night a year. According to the spell, if someone would stay married to me as a frog for three months, the spell would break. My time would have been up at midnight. You have burned my frog skin one hour too soon!

Ivan: Please forgive me, Vasilisa. I will do anything to break the spell.

Vasilisa: Quickly then, meet me at the house of Baba-Yaga. She is the only one who can help.

Narrator: Then Vasilisa clapped her hands. Her white gown turned into soft feathers. She became a swan and flew out the window. Ivan watched in amazement. Then he set off to find the house of Baba-Yaga.

amazement   wonder or surprise

Ivan: (*nervously*) Baba-Yaga, I have come for your help. I'm looking for Vasilisa.

Baba-Yaga: Your frog wife is trapped by a spell. You can help free her by following this advice. (*Singing*)

> Should you see some swamp creatures,
> Catch them. Hold them.
> Do not let them free.
> Should you grasp an arrow,
> Snap it on your knee!

Narrator: Just then, a white swan flew up to Baba-Yaga's hut. Ivan knew the swan was Vasilisa, and he caught it in his arms. The swan's feathers fell to the ground, and Ivan was left holding a frog.

Ivan: Don't wriggle, Vasilisa!

Narrator: No sooner had Ivan spoken than the frog turned into a flapping mudfish. Then the slippery fish became a twisting weasel. Ivan held on tight. Next, the weasel turned into a slithery swamp snake. Finally, the snake turned into an arrow.

Ivan: My arrow! Baba-Yaga said that if I should grasp an arrow, I should snap it on my knee, so that is what I will do. (*Ivan snaps the arrow, and Vasilisa reappears.*)

wriggle to twist or turn

Vasilisa: My brave and kind Ivan, you have set me free!

Ivan: My princess! You are a frog no longer. I have broken the spell at last.

Narrator: In time, Prince Ivan and Princess Vasilisa became Czar Ivan and Czarina Vasilisa, and, of course, they lived happily ever after!

Discussion Starters

1　Why did the czar say that Prince Ivan had to marry the frog?

2　How do you think the other characters will treat Vasilisa now that she is a beautiful princess and not an ugly frog?

At what points in the story do you think Prince Ivan shows kindness to the Frog Princess?